"HELLO READING books are a perfect introduction to reading. Brief sentences full of word repetition and full-color pictures stress visual clues to help a child take the first important steps toward reading. Mastering these story books will build children's reading confidence and give them the enthusiasm to stand on their own in the world of words."

—Bee Cullinan
Past President of the International Reading
Association, Professor in New York University's
Early Childhood and Elementary Education Program

"Readers aren't born, they're made. Desire is planted—planted by parents who work at it."

—Jim Trelease
author of *The Read Aloud Handbook*

"When I was a classroom reading teacher, I recognized the importance of good stories in making children understand that reading is more than just recognizing words. I saw that children who have ready access to story books get excited about reading. They also make noticeably greater gains in reading comprehension. The development of the HELLO READING stories grows out of this experience."

—Harriet Ziefert
M.A.T., New York University School of Education
Author, Language Arts Module,
Scholastic Early Childhood Program

For Jason and Lucy
S.T.

PUFFIN BOOKS
Viking Penguin Inc., 40 West 23rd Street,
New York, New York 10010, U.S.A.
Penguin Books Ltd., Harmondsworth, Middlesex, England
Penguin Books Australia Ltd., Ringwood, Victoria, Australia
Penguin Books Canada Limited, 2801 John St., Markham, Ontario, Canada
Penguin Books (N.Z.) Ltd., 182–190 Wairau Rd., Auckland 10, New Zealand

First published in 1987
3   5   7   9   10   8   6   4
Text copyright © Harriet Ziefert, 1987
Illustrations copyright © Simms Taback, 1987

Jason's Bus Ride

Harriet Ziefert
Illustrated by Simms Taback

PUFFIN BOOKS

Jason got on the bus.

He paid the bus driver.

Then he found a good seat.

Jason looked around.

There were all kinds
of people on the bus.

There were all kinds
of people outside.

Jason saw cars and trucks
and bikes and motorcycles.

All of a sudden
the bus stopped.

"Why did we stop?"
Jason asked.

A man said, "The bus stopped
because of a dog. The dog
is in front of the bus."

The dog would not move.
He would not get out
of the way.

The bus driver
beeped his horn.

But the dog would not
get out of the way!

A lady shouted,
"Shoo! Shoo!"

But the dog would not
get out of the way!

A policeman
blew his whistle.

But the dog would not
get out of the way!

A man and a lady
pulled the dog.

But the dog would not
get out of the way!

A lady with a crying baby
walked up to the dog.

The lady said, "Move away!
My baby wants to go home."

But the dog would not
get out of the way!

Everyone watched.
Everyone waited.

Jason patted the dog.
Good dog! Good dog!

The dog smiled.

Then he walked away.

Jason got back on the bus.